W9-BLS-612

You've watched and you've wondered and waited all year for the **day** of all days to finally be here!

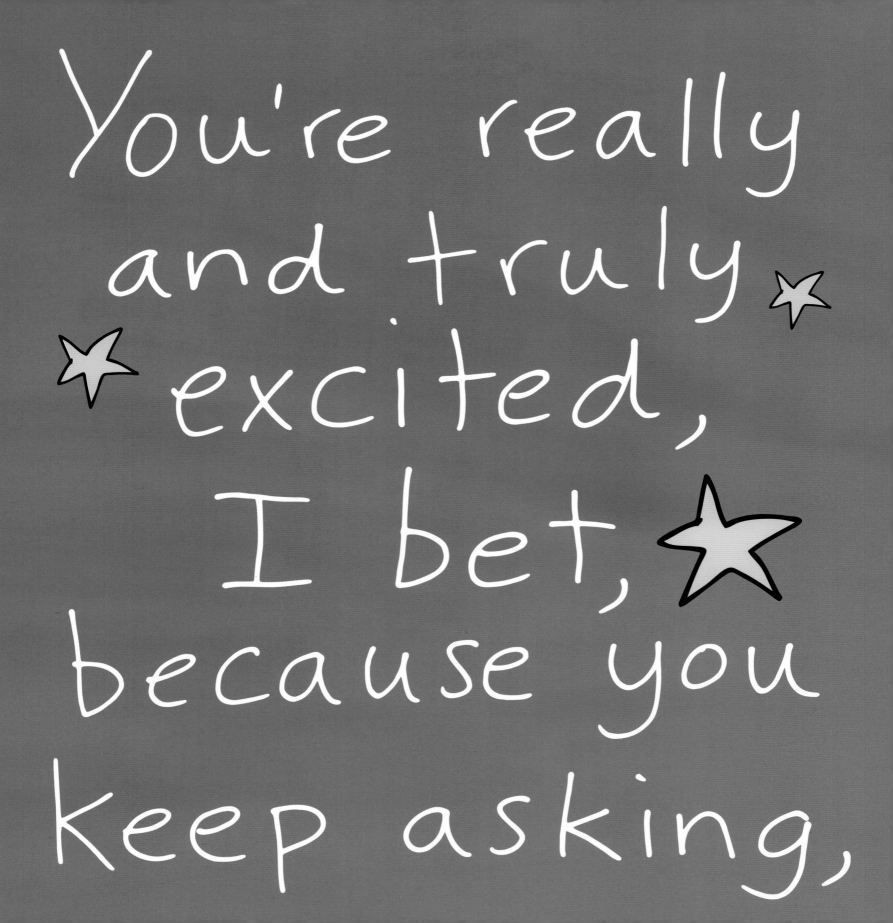

You're really
and truly
excited,
I bet,
because you
keep asking,

So, how will you know if Christmas is here? You'll just have to answer some **questions,** my dear!

Is your house filled with goodies and Christmas cards? Do you see **snowmen** smiling in lots of yards?

Is there a tree in your house with a star on the top? Do you think Santa's busy making **toys** in his shop?

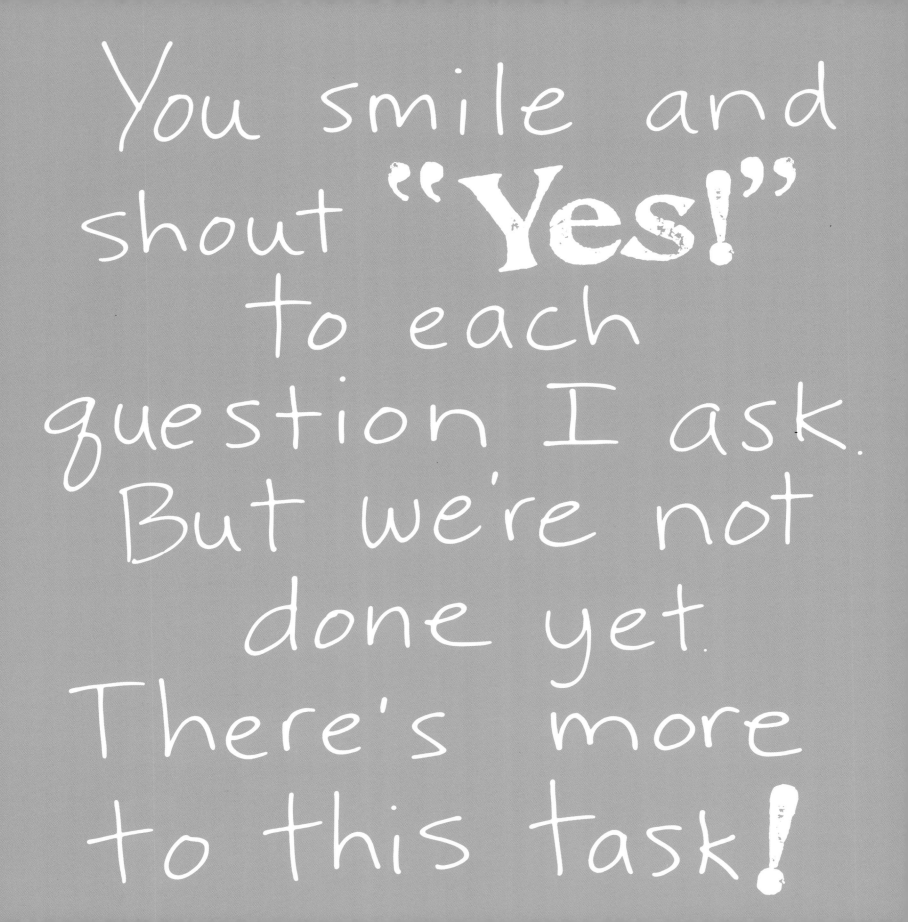

Have you looked at the stars that fill up the sky? Do you think that you've seen Santa's **reindeer** fly by?

Have your friends and family come from faraway places? Have you made lots of **gingerbread** cookies with big, funny faces?

So many
happen at this
each is a
Chris
is

magical things
time of year, and
clue that
tmas
near!

Of course, **Santa** will come, leaving gifts by the tree, but that's not **who** makes Christmas, at least not to me!

It's **YOU!**
You're the star
that lights up
my days.
You're my gift and
my blessing, in so
many ways!

You put the **merry** in Merry Christmas, my precious one. You fill my world with giggles, laughter and tons of fun!

You see, Christmas is more than one day in December. It's the time spent **together** that we'll always remember.

Now, there's just one little thing ✫ left to do, and that's to ✫ **answer** the question for you! ✫

Text and illustrations © 2016 Hanny Girl Productions, Inc. www.sandramagsamen.com
Exclusively represented by Mixed Media Group, Inc. NY, NY.
Cover and internal design © 2016 by Sandra Magsamen

Sourcebooks and the colophon are registered trademarks of Sourcebooks, Inc.

All rights reserved. No part of this book may be reproduced in any form or by any electronic or
mechanical means including information storage and retrieval systems—except in the case of
brief quotations embodied in critical articles or reviews—without permission in writing from its
publisher, Sourcebooks, Inc.

Published by Sourcebooks Jabberwocky, an imprint of Sourcebooks, Inc.
P.O. Box 4410, Naperville, Illinois 60567-4410
(630) 961-3900
Fax: (630) 961-2168
www.sourcebooks.com

Library of Congress Cataloging-in-Publication data is on file with the publisher.

Source of Production: Leo Paper, Heshan City, Guangdong Province, China
Date of Production: June 2016
Run Number: 5006764

Printed and bound in China.
LEO 10 9 8 7 6 5 4 3 2 1